Pets

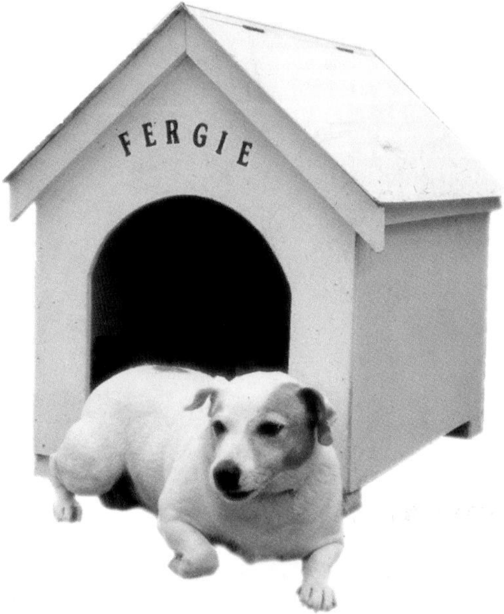

The cat is here.

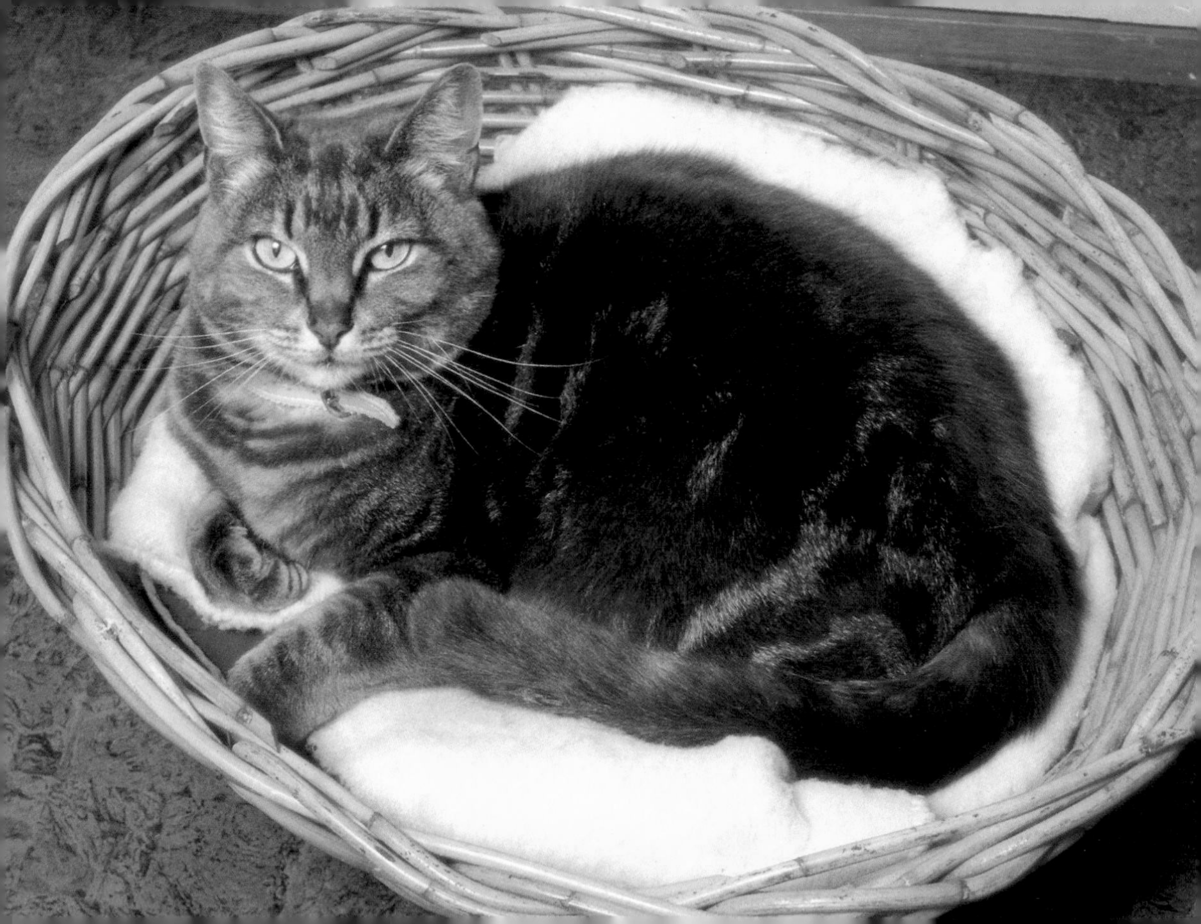

The dog is here.

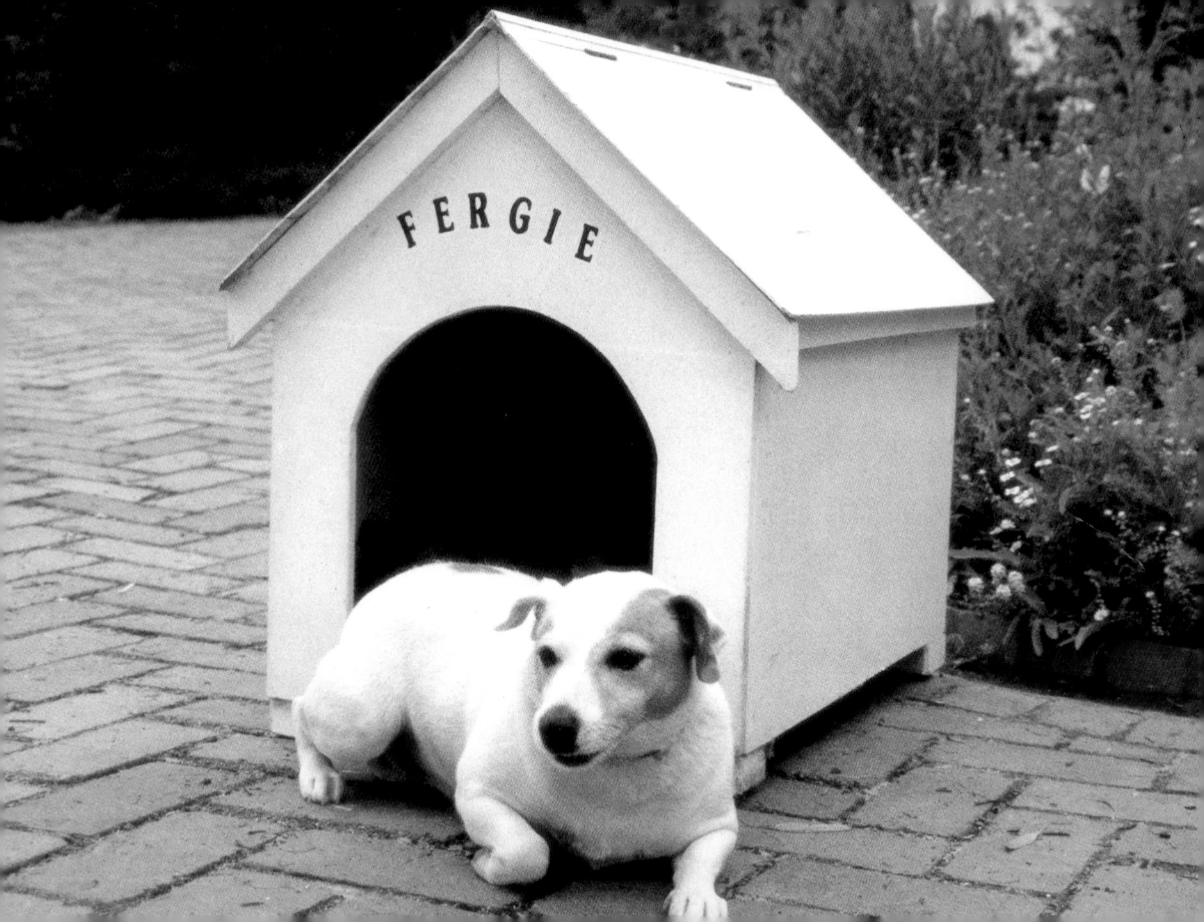
FERGIE

The bird is here.

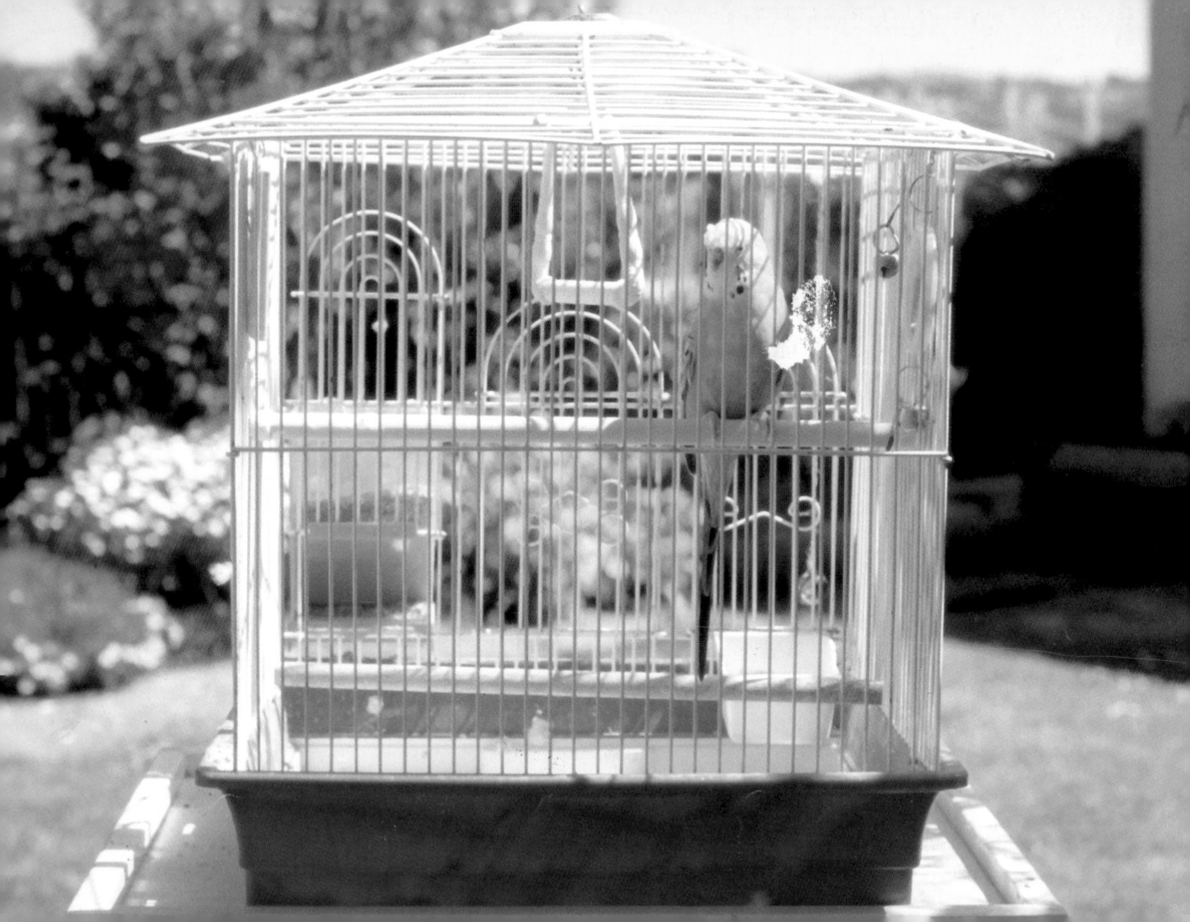

The rabbit is here.

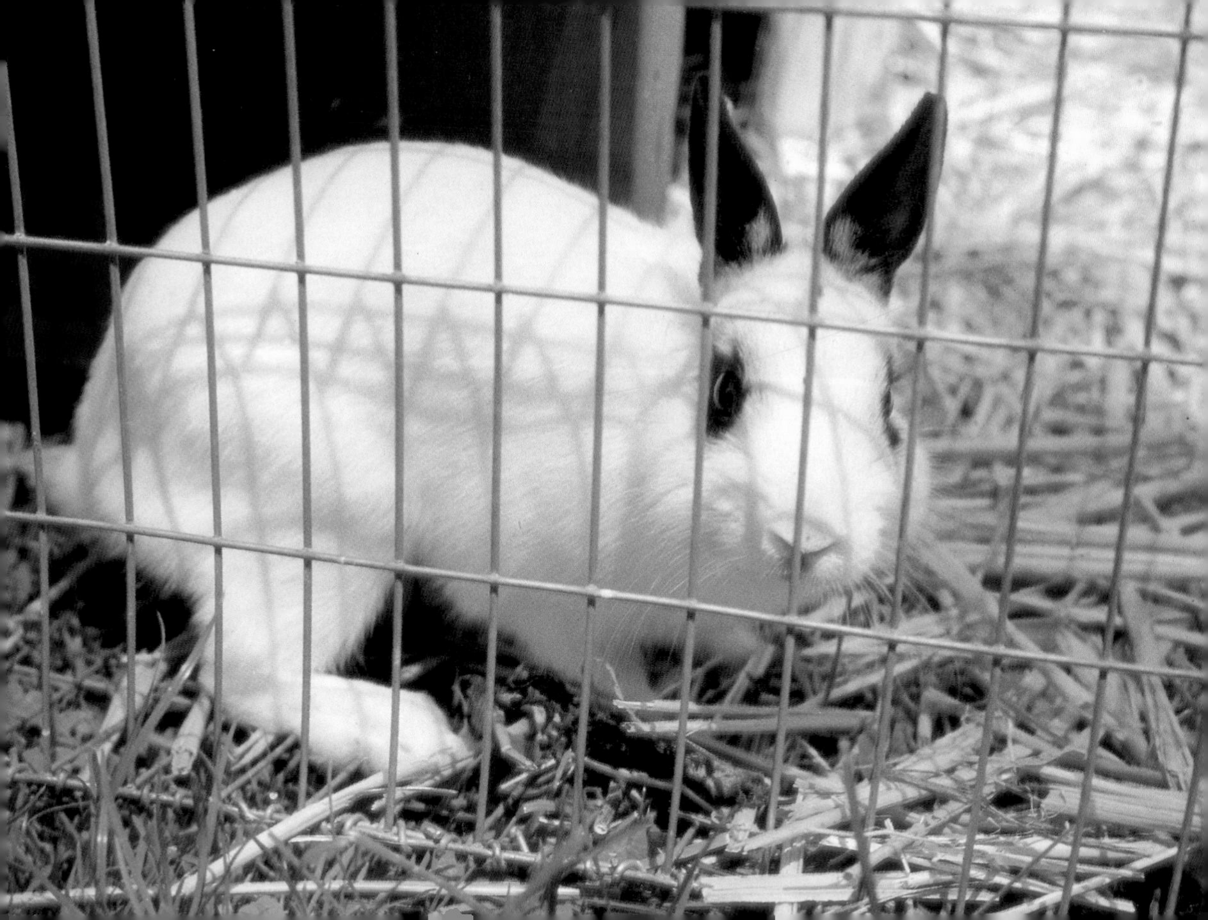

The goldfish is here.

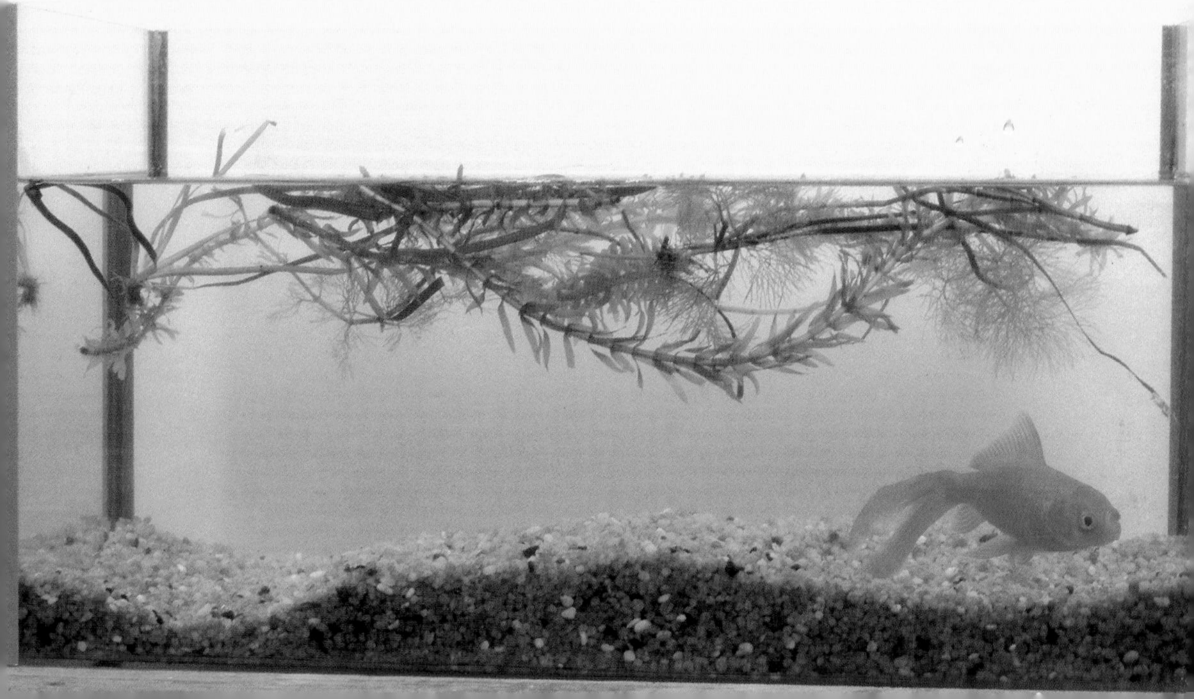

The mouse is here.

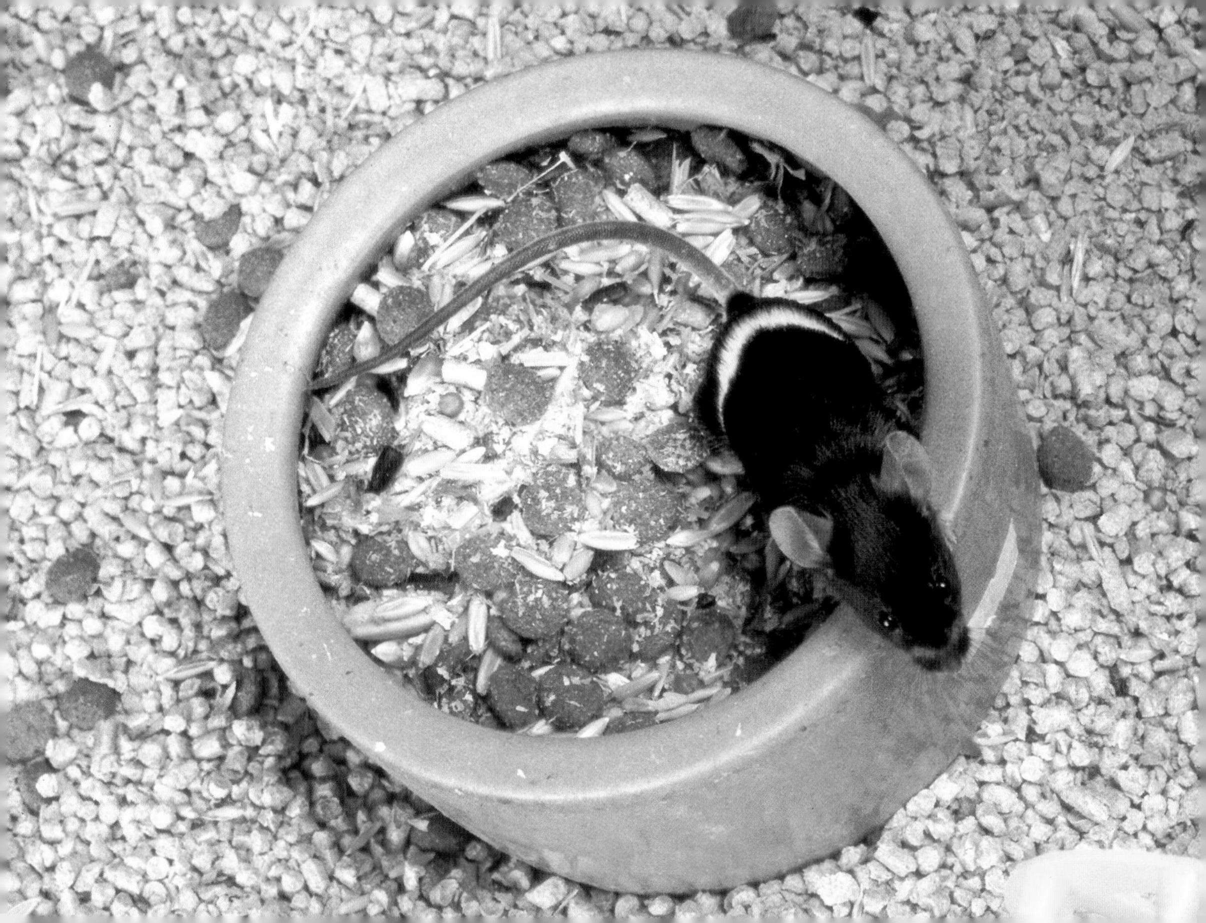

The guinea pig is here.

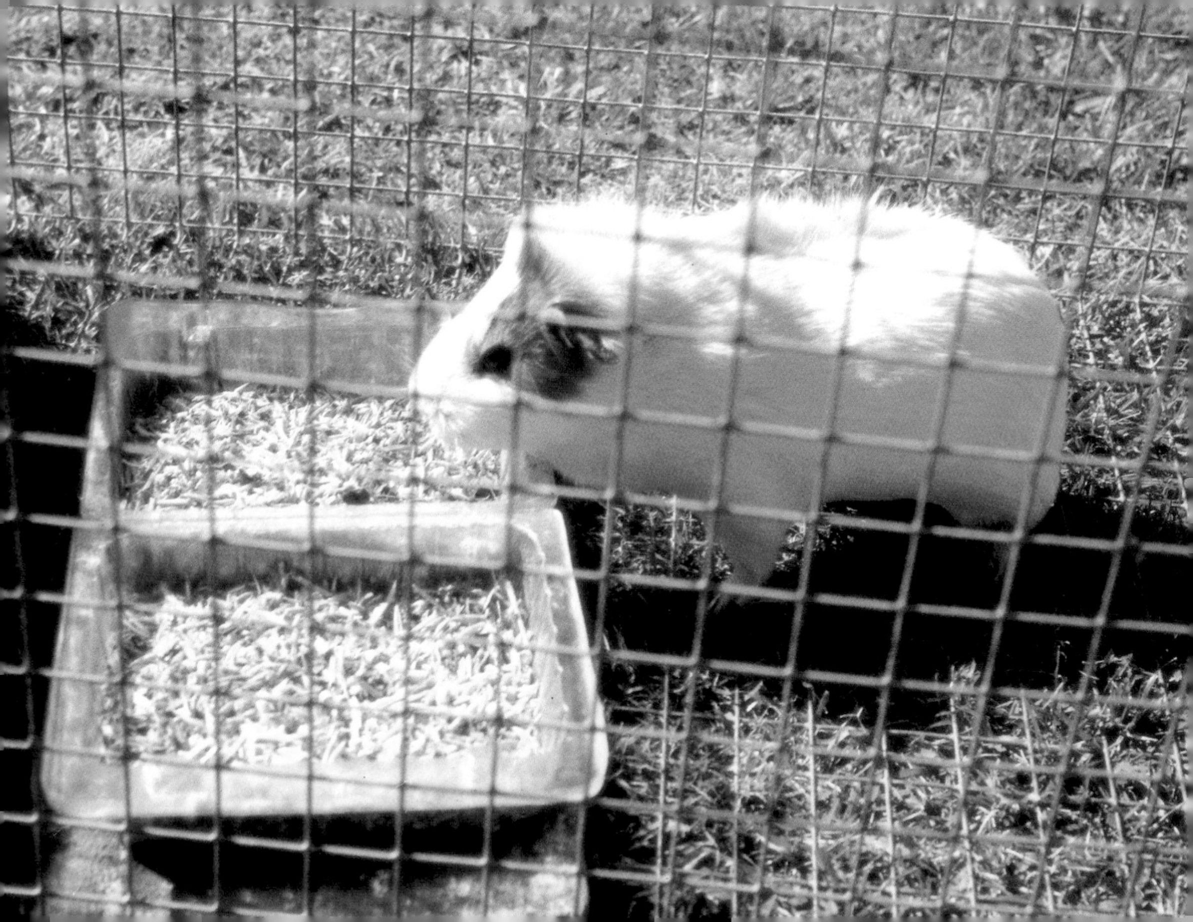

The turtle is here.

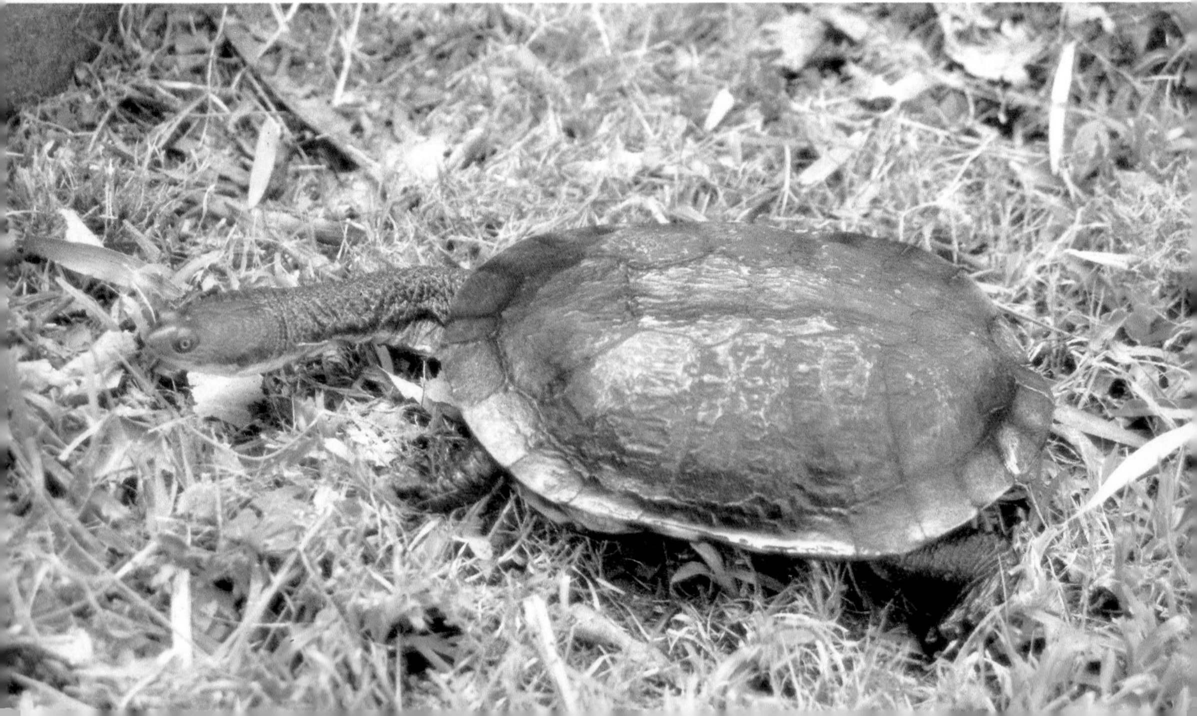